MW00973459

For my blue sky, Kristen, and my sunny days, Lilly, Anna Jane and Jack. – J.M.

For Rachel, Luke, Jack and Levi. – J.B.

Copyright © 2015 by Greenville Health System

All rights reserved. This book or any portion thereof may not be reproduced or used in any manner whatsoever without the express written permission of the publisher except for the use of brief quotations in a book review.

Printed in the United States of America
Printed by e**media**group, inc.

Second Printing, 2016

Library of Congress Control Number: 2015936501
ISBN: 978-0-692-41058-5

Published by Greenville Health System

www.goodnightgreenville.com

Book designed by Steven Serek and edited by Jeanine Halva-Neubauer

Goodnight Greenville

Written by Joe Maurer
Illustrated by Joseph Bradley

Goodnight
Falls Park

Goodnight
Swamp Rabbit
Trail

Goodnight
Fluor Field
and bats that
are swung

Goodnight
Children's Theatre, drama and laughs

Goodnight Greenville Zoo
and lions that roar

Goodnight Children's Museum
and rooms to explore

Goodnight Children's Garden, flowers and bees

Goodnight Paris Mountain, trails, lakes and trees

Goodnight Downtown Greenville

and trolleys on wheels

Goodnight Children's Hospital and families it heals

Goodnight Greenville,
Gem of the Upstate

Located in downtown Greenville, **Falls Park on the Reedy** (River) was founded in 1967 when Carolina Foothills Garden Club reclaimed 26 acres from textile mills. In the late 1990s and early 2000s, Mayor Knox White directed significant revitalization of the park, including construction of the nationally acclaimed Liberty Bridge and beautification of 20 acres of public gardens. Both the bridge and the park have won numerous awards.

Greenville Health System Swamp Rabbit Trail is an ever-expanding greenway system that covers much of Greenville County. The paved trail largely follows a former railroad bed nicknamed after the indigenous swamp rabbit. It debuted in 2010 and is traveled by over 400,000 people annually on bike or foot.

Fluor Field at the West End is home to the Greenville Drive, a minor-league baseball team for the Boston Red Sox. Field dimensions replicate Boston's famous Fenway Park and includes a version of the Green Monster in left field and "Pesky's Pole" in right. The stadium opened its gates in 2006.

The **Peace Center** presented its first curtain call in 1990 on the site of three former factories in downtown Greenville. It includes a 2,100-seat concert hall and the 400-seat Dorothy Hipp Gunter Theatre. The center houses four companies: Greenville Symphony Orchestra, Carolina Ballet Theatre, South Carolina Children's Theatre and the International Ballet. It hosts over 600 events each year, many nationally acclaimed.

TD Saturday Market is an open-air farmers market that features locally grown products (plants, meats, honey), prepared foods, arts, crafts and entertainment. It runs Saturday mornings from May to October in downtown Greenville. Begun in 2002, the market moved to its current location on Main Street in 2007.

The **South Carolina Children's Theatre** is an award-winning organization that has entertained for over 25 years. It presents several in-house productions a year, many performed at the Peace Center. It also offers extensive educational and outreach opportunities.

The **Greenville Zoo** is a 14-acre facility that opened in 1960. It is home to many animal species, including rare African lions. It attracts 270,000 visitors annually and boasts a children's program and many special events.

The **Children's Museum of the Upstate** has educated children since 2009. Every year, over 20,000 students enjoy its hands-on programs. The 10th largest children's museum in the world, it also is the country's only Smithsonian-affiliated children's museum. The expansive facility houses three floors of activities, including an exhibition hall that attracts national showcases.

The Children's Garden at Linky Stone Park is a 1.7-acre park tucked along the Reedy River in downtown Greenville amid the Greenville Health System Swamp Rabbit Trail. The hands-on park provides an opportunity for kids to learn about their natural world.

 Paris Mountain State Park consists of 1,540 acres offering biking, hiking, boating, camping and other outdoor activities. Its 2,000-foot peak overlooks the city of Greenville. Open year-round, the park holds a summer concert series and many ongoing children's activities.

 After downtown Greenville began to languish in the mid-1900s, it underwent a significant revitalization starting in the 1980s. In recent years, it has grown to become a popular destination for food, music and entertainment. The **Downtown Trolley** is free, runs all year and stops at all of the popular downtown attractions.

 **Children's Hospital of Greenville Health System** is the Upstate's only hospital recognized by the national Children's Hospital Association. It provides leading-edge therapies while delivering "whole child" care to over 360,000 patients a year. Signature services include a 24-hour ER staffed by pediatric specialists, 80-bed neonatal ICU, cancer center, the area's sole pediatric rheumatology division and several renowned specialty programs.

 **Roper Mountain Science Center** has provided educational opportunities since 1985. The center holds multiple programs and camps for many ages, including weekly Friday Starry Nights, a cosmic exploration in the planetarium with the nation's eighth largest refractor telescope. It also operates a popular light display during the holiday season, along with regular events for both children and adults.

 **Greenville, South Carolina**, long part of Cherokee hunting grounds, was founded in 1831. Known as the "Textile Center of the World" in the early 1900s, today's Greenville combines Southern charm, natural beauty and contemporary cool, making it a popular travel destination. Nestled in the foothills of the Blue Ridge Mountains, this jewel of a city features a revitalized downtown with one-of-a-kind bridge, quaint shops, sophisticated restaurants, enterprising businesses, respected educational institutions, vibrant arts scene and renowned museums. The area also boasts some of the country's most scenic landscapes. Greenville truly is the "Gem of the Upstate"!

Joe Maurer, MD, is a writer and a pediatrician with Greenville Health System. He lives in Greenville with his wife, Kristen, and their three children: Lilly, Anna Jane and Jack.

Joseph Bradley is an award-winning, nationally recognized artist. He lives in Greenville with wife Rachel and their three children: Luke, Jack and Levi.